Raavana's Daughter

by Nadishka Aloysius
Illustrated by Vasika Udurawane

ISBN-13: 978-955-51847-7-9

The most haunting time at which to see them is at the turn of the moon, when they utter strange wailing cries; but the lagoon is dangerous for mortals then...

- J. M. Barrie, Peter Pan

I have heard the mermaids singing, each to each.
I do not think that they will sing to me.
I have seen them riding seaward on the waves
Combing the white hair of the waves blown back
When the wind blows the water white and black.
We have lingered in the chambers of the sea
By sea-girls wreathed with seaweed red and brown
Till human voices wake us, and we drown.

— T.S Eliot, The Love Song of J. Alfred Prufrock

iv

PROLOGUE

Raavana, the Demon King, has abducted Sita, Rama's wife. She is held captive in the hill country of Raavana's kingdom in Lanka. Rama, the Prince of Ayodya, has convinced the Ape Men, known as the Vanara, to assist him in his quest to win her freedom.

Hanuman, the greatest of Ape heroes discovers the exact location of Sita's imprisonment. He is then instructed to build a bridge from South India to Lanka, so that Rama's invading army can cross the Palk Strait, and rescue the kidnapped princess.

However, little does he suspect that all is not as it seems. Dangers that lurk in the depths of the ocean will test his resilience and loyalty...

CHAPTER ONE

The greenish-grey waters closest to the shore of Pamban Island were already at war with the deeper turquoise-blue expanse bordering them. Little waves lapped at the pebbled shore, while larger ones crested in the distance, biding their time. Eddies and swirls danced across the surface to the magical music of the Indian Ocean. The air smelt unsullied and devoid of the heaviness he had

had to endure in the jungle. The refreshing briny taste was already on his lips just one day into the expedition. The wind had picked up since the war party had arrived the day before and pennants which had hung limp now flapped and tugged with a vengeance.

Hanuman stood barefoot at the water's edge. The shaggy brown fur that covered him stirred in the gusting wind. His leather armour was barely visible as its colour blended seamlessly into the earthy colours gifted him by nature. The commander of the Vanara army surveyed the scenery, but its beauty did not enthral him, since his mind was elsewhere, on actions past. He clenched his massive fists, as a fire raged in his veins, and he reflected on the indignities he had had to suffer leading up to this moment. With a shake of his head Hanuman pushed those thoughts aside. "Time enough for that, later," he chided himself. "Now, I must figure out how to transport an army of Vanara and

Humans across to defeat the enemy on their own soil."

Raavana's domain was a murky haze in the horizon. The jagged ends of mountains could be seen above the thin mist as if to warn unwanted travellers away from the Demon's homeland. The land was close enough that shrieks and hoots of wild animals would carry across the water when nights were still. Hanuman knew although he and his Vanara army could leap across the Straight which divided South India and Lanka, the Humans were in need of assistance.

He respected Lord Rama, and understood his determination and his plight. He had undertaken the task of locating Sita and her abductor without a second thought; and he regretted none of his actions. "However," reflected Hanuman wryly, "if I had known I would have to brandish a torch tied to my tail, and build bridges, I may have not given my consent!" The thought was fleeting, and without rancour, and accompanied by a smile.

He turned his back on the green-blue empty landscape as he headed back into the camp. It was time to plan the invasion.

Hanuman strode through the camp. As he walked he took in the hustle and bustle of an army greeting a new day. Camp fires were lit, and assorted smells of cooking drifted in the air mingling with the more earthy smells of horses, Apes and Humans. He headed for his command tent which was erected in the centre. Neela was nominally Commander-in-Chief of the Vanara army, but he had given the fore to Hanuman since he had spied out the land.

He swept back the canvas sheets and entered. The tent was functional and sparsely furnished. As the sun had yet to fully greet the day, lamps had been lit and the walls of the tent were decorated with dancing shadows. Those gathered around the centre table were poring over diagrams and discussing strategy. "What is there left to argue about?" wondered Hanuman, as he joined them, "the decision to build a bridge has already been made, and approved, by Lord Rama." Of course, he knew that although Neela and Nala respected each other and worked well together, they could not share a room without igniting into discussion.

This discussion revolved around the engineering problems they faced in regard to the bridge. Neela was asserting his opinion that the Strait s were deeper than they seemed and that the demand for rocks and timber would be too great. He held the view that they needed something more if they were to make the crossing safe and swift.

Hanuman looked at Nala standing resolutely at the other end of the table. Nala was the Chief Engineer and Architect of the Vanara army. "As I have said since we began this project, I am confident my workers can ferry timber sufficient for the task! We are on an island, yes, but within stone's throw of Tamil Nadu and her lush forests. We can easily transport the wood we need for a bridge. There is enough limestone rock already on this island. My Apes are skilled, they will build your bridge!"

"Sticks and stones do not make a bridge!" Neela snorted. "The Strait is no puddle! It is deep enough to house sea creatures in many forms. Tell me, Nala, if you have made precise calculations as to demand and supply?"

"Well, really..." spluttered Nala, but Hanuman raised a hand. Everyone directed their gaze at him; he was expected to give the final verdict. "We will start to build it as Nala suggests. He is the architect of our Majesty's vast halls, and I have faith in him. However, this is no ordinary war we fight. Raavana is a Demon. He may resort to supernatural means to stop us. I will consider this more; but we need to begin. Lord Rama will tolerate no delay on our part."

With that the assembly dispersed, each to see to his own tasks.

CHAPTER TWO

Following the day's exertions, Hanuman assigned the guards their duty and sought his bed in his private tent. He had been preoccupied the entire day, his thoughts on the safety and durability of the bridge. Yet, he did not want to inconvenience Lord Rama with his worries. His thoughts drifted into sleep as he considered a variety of possibilities.

Within seconds he was dreaming. He was floating above the waters of the Strait . However, unlike that morning, the waves were now churning and leaping higher and higher. In his dream Hanuman became afraid that he would be dragged down to the depths of the ocean. Then, he glimpsed an azure light building to his right. He could just glimpse it out of the corner of his eye. Then it blazed and night became day in a flood of light. The waves were suddenly still, as if in anticipation of what was to come next.

Out of the calm sea rose the head of a beast. It had a cavernous mouth lined with jagged teeth the length of a man's arm. Scaly like a crocodile, but with the hind quarters of a seal it thrashed the waves as it moved towards him. Hanuman recognized Makara the vehicle of the God Varuna. He found himself hurtling through the air, right up to the beast's mouth.

"Why do you summon me?" thundered a voice out of the blinding light.

"I?" inquired Hanuman. "I do not summon you, great Lord Varuna!"

"Your anxiety ridden thoughts have been as sharp barbs in my mind this whole day!" barked the God of the Ocean. "If you wish a boon, speak!"

Hanuman considered his words, choosing with care what he would say. He did not wish to anger the one God who would be their strongest ally.

"My Lord," he said, "you already know my thoughts. My doubts. You know that we are here at the bidding of Lord Rama. You know what is at stake. I would be eternally grateful if you could provide some assistance in the fording of this waterway. I did not voice my misgivings to the others, but how many trees will we need to tear down? How much of the cliff face and the shoreline will we have to deface to get the material we need? I do not wish to cause so much harm…"

"You speak well, Son of the Apes," replied Varuna. "Therefore, I will grant you one boon —write the name of Rama on the boulders you find on the shores of this island. Throw them into the water. They will float. You can use what timber you have to steady the bridge."

Hanuman was sceptical, "Floating bridge?" he thought, but said, "Thank you! Oh Great God of the Waters! The Lady Sita is fortunate that you assist us in our journey towards her!"

Varuna did not wait on any ceremony, but disappeared back into the light.

Hanuman considered what had been said. Construction would indeed speed up if they required only the boulders to form the surface of the bridge. He

closed his eyes, expecting to return to his bed. Yet, when he reopened them and looked around he found himself still hovering over the water. "This is obviously a dream," he told himself, "yet why am I still here?"

A white mist rose out of the waves, and in a few seconds had obscured his vision. This was accompanied by a hum that seemed to pierce his whole being. He felt his skin prickle and his hair stand on end. The sound developed into a wordless song that washed over him like the very waves of the ocean.

Then he noticed a golden sheen on the water below him. The light seemed to be searing out from the depths. The waves were breaking into what looked like small pieces of oddly shaped glass. The glass merged to form the tail end of an enormous fish. The light reflecting off it splintered into all the hues of the rainbow. Light and song caught him in a whirlwind that buffeted him like a ragdoll left and right.

As suddenly as it began, it stopped. In the eerie calm that followed, Hanuman gazed in awe at the colours, wondering what this could mean. Was it a warning of something else to come? He was so engrossed in the lights that he did not notice the tail lifting out of the water. The powerful blow which followed flung him into the air – and back into his bed, his ears filled with a woman's soft laughter.

He awoke with a start, a soreness on his right side, where the blow had struck. Pulling back the sheets he inspected the wound. There was a purple bruise where no bruise should be. And then, before his watching eyes, it faded, into nothing.

CHAPTER THREE

Hanuman awoke to the sound of horns in the dawn, calling all workers to their appointed tasks. He met with the other leaders of the army as soon as breakfast was done, and shared with them Lord Varuna's promise. Neela accepted the news saying, "We are fortunate a God is on our side!"

However, Nala, frowned. "I do not disbelieve your message that Lord Varuna will intercede for us. Yet, as an engineer, I find it difficult to accept that floating rocks will be sufficient to get us across! We have horses, chariots and equipment that will need to be hauled on those rocks. If they are not steady, everything will end up in the Makara's mouth!"

Hanuman smiled. This was as he had expected. Nala was too practical minded to blindly jump at a God's command. "I too would like a demonstration of how this will work. Let us go to the shore and throw a few rocks to test the theory!"

A large crowd had gathered at the water's edge. "Even dreams do not stay secret anymore," noted Hanuman as he surveyed the crowd. Nala had collected his strongest workers near some large limestone rocks.

They had the ability to toss the boulders into the deeper part of the Strait . Hanuman approached them as they prepared for their task. He bent and traced the name RAMA on each boulder. He watched as they lifted the rocks onto their backs, muscles bulging. Then with a tremendous heave the rocks were flying through the air, their aim straight and true. They landed with a spectacular splash some distance away. Hanuman took out his eye-glass. Nala and Neela were already peering through theirs.

The rocks sank below the waves.

They glanced at each other, as a ripple of whispers passed through those watching the demonstration.

Then, silence.

The wind which had been gusting through the crowd had ceased. It was as if the whole world collectively held its breath.

"Look!" shouted one of the onlookers.

All heads whipped towards the ocean. A gentle swirl could be seen where the rocks had landed. The circular motion widened until it resembled a minor whirlpool. The water seemed to get sucked in and then, as suddenly as it happened, it stopped. Where the churning water had been, there were now a cluster of rocks, floating on the ocean.

The silence was broken by applause and the excited chatter of Human and Vanara.

Hanuman turned to Nala and said, "That dispels any doubt, surely? Lord Varuna knows how to engineer a spectacle!"

Nala looked back, ecstasy and excitement dancing across his face. He pounded Hanuman's shoulder in his enthusiasm. "Yes!" he exclaimed, "and now, to work!"

The rest of the day flew past. Both Human and Vanara workers dove into their tasks with a zeal that reflected the wonder of Lord Varuna's promise. The Humans cut and transported the rocks to the sea shore, while the Vanara heaved them into the water. They built up a rhythm that was mesmerizing to watch. Wooden planks were brought from the mainland to bind the rocks together. By nightfall more than half the distance to Lanka had been covered, and everyone sought their beds satisfied with what had been accomplished.

The ocean is our slave...

It will soon be their grave...

Then will we all swim free...

What is promised will soon be...

CHAPTER FOUR

Hanuman did not dream that night, but slept fitfully, tossing and turning until the bedclothes resembled the whirlpool of the previous day. He awoke with a feeling of unease at the back of his mind. As a seasoned warrior and commander he was accustomed to such jolts from his subconscious. He dressed for the day, and as he was lacing his boots he realized the dawn call had not sounded as yet. It was obviously well into the day and Hanuman hurried out, weapon in hand, to see what could have gone wrong on a well-guarded but deserted island.

The camp was eerily quiet, with only the occasional whinny of a horse or stamp of a hoof. There were no cooking fires today, no workers running about, just a sleepy stillness. The pennants hung limp as if awaiting the awakening of the slumbering army.

Hanuman gripped his sword and exited his tent. His guards were nowhere to be seen. He crept through the camp, on alert for anything else out of the ordinary. He first made his way to Neela's tent. The guards were asleep on their feet. He flicked a hand before their faces, but received no reaction. He stealthily entered the tent. Neela, too, was still asleep. Hanuman strode up to the bed and shook him awake. "Warriors sleep lightly," he thought as he slapped Neela's face, "this must be the work of Raavana. Demon magic." He was finally able to awaken the sleeping commander. Together they worked their way through the rest of the camp. Hanuman noted how, even though the noise and bustle resumed, every single person had to be shaken awake, as if unable to regain consciousness on their own.

After the camp had been scoured for any threat, and the perimeters double checked, everyone was put back to work. The commanders gathered to debate their next move.

"What CAN we do?" demanded Nala. "We are at war with a Demon. We have no magic of our own to counter that! The guards were snoring where they stood! We must manage as best we can!"

"I will NOT be murdered in my bed like a babe!" countered Neela. "We may have survived last night unscathed, but the attack may be more vicious next time!"

Hanuman intervened before the argument could grow. "Our healers may have some herbs that can counter drowsiness and make one more alert. We can distribute a pouch to each person and command that they carry it with them at all times. We can also be more alert; whoever cast the spell may have approached in a boat..."

Nala cut him off with a snort. "We are battling a crazed Demon! He would not need a boat!"

They were interrupted by a messenger who stumbled into the tent.

"My lords!" he gasped. "The bridge... it's gone!"

They all rushed to the shoreline to confirm this disturbing news. The bridge which had reached halfway across the Strait yesterday, had indeed vanished.

Hanuman and the other commanders summoned all those who were on guard the previous night. Each person had a similar tale to tell. They remembered very little of what had happened; a sudden feeling of excessive fatigue followed by obliviousness. One or two however, recalled a haunting melody in the night, soft and alluring. When asked to pinpoint the origin of the sound, they said it seemed to seep out of the water. One Vanara who had been on watch by the shore, claimed to have seen silver fish in a dream. Yet, he was the only one to have dreamt at all that night.

Hanuman was troubled. He remembered clearly his own premonition. This was no mere coincidence. Something malevolent was in the water, and if left unconquered, it could lead them to their doom.

Rip and tear, bend and break...

A bridge to Lanka they will not make...

Splash and twirl, heave and hurl...

All their plans will now unfurl...

CHAPTER FIVE

That night, Hanuman did not prepare for bed. Instead as darkness swallowed the land he wore his armour and waited for a repetition of the enchantment of the night before. He was certain it would reoccur, since the bridge had been rebuilt. The objective of the spell casters was obviously to hinder their efforts to cross the Strait .

As promised, he had ordered that a pouch of herbs be distributed to everyone, and he clutched his in his hand as he waited. The aroma of the leaves and flowers crushed in his grasp was sufficient to drive away all need to sleep. The hours stretched long and at midnight he decided to take his watch to the sea shore.

He nodded to the guards posted outside his tent as he passed by, and checked on the night watch. When he was halfway through the camp, it began.

First, a pale silvery glow emanated from the direction of the ocean. Hanuman knew it was not the moon since this was a new moon night. Then, the sound of the splashing waves grew louder. This was followed by voices raised in song - but in a harmony that was simultaneously beautiful and jarring to the ear. It had an ethereal quality, hypnotic and obviously supernatural. The voices merged in a chorus that may have never before been heard by Human or Ape. A sudden crash to his right made him swivel, sword held high. All he saw was one of the guards lying prone on the ground. This was the mysterious musical spell that had overcome them last night.

The music pressed down on his eyelids, forcing them closed, and his feet felt as though they were turned to stone. He dropped down on all fours and rested his head on the hand that still clutched the pouch. "Now we will see if these concoctions really work," thought Hanuman as he inhaled deeply. It took a few disoriented moments, but he soon felt the stupor lift a little. He crawled back into his tent and hunted for some scraps of leather he knew were on the table. Working fast he rolled the leather as tight and small as he could and stuffed them into his ears. The relief was immediate. Once the sound was blocked out, the fog in his mind lifted and he was able to reason again. He emerged from the tent, ready for any attack; but there was none. The light was still visible from the seashore, and Hanuman raced passed sleeping guards towards the bridge.

The silver glow originated in the water itself. Running along the shore Hanuman noticed how it was not a steady light, but it seemed to pulse and change colour, beating a rhythm that accompanied the eerie music. At times it seemed to glint as if off scales of fish. His mind immediately turned to his dream, and the giant fish that had attacked him. He slowed down so as not to draw attention to himself and crawled the last few spans, hiding behind the limestone outcroppings.

The bridge was partially demolished already. Whoever was responsible for this attack, was efficient and worked fast. As he watched, a chunk of stone was wrenched off the wooden beams and thrust into the water. It did not re-emerge. So, they had powers equivalent to those of Rama and Varuna to so easily brush aside the spell of buoyancy. That was when he noticed that the arms tearing the rocks apart were humanoid hands, pale and thin. He clutched his sword, his thoughts whirring in disbelief. No Human was capable of such a feat. Now that he knew what to watch out for, he was able to spot many pairs of hands, working in tandem, attacking the rocks. Then, he saw hair - if it could be called that - matted and long, like seaweed, framing a face which was most definitely not Human. It was pointed, the bone structure angular, the skin luminescent. The eyes were reptilian slits. The nose two flat holes set in the face.

Hanuman had never seen the creatures but he had heard tales of ships being lured to their destruction by their song -

Mermaids!

Seaweed coats our lustrous hair...

Our lives we live without a care...

Sailors learn to tread with fear...

The Mer-folk own the ocean here..

CHAPTER SIX

Hanuman was appalled to see Mermaids active in the ocean around the island. There was no record of them inhabiting the waters of South India, and no seamen had reported a sighting - which, of course, did not mean they did not exist. Quickly, Hanuman formulated a plan. He was on his own. He needed to gather intelligence about the creatures in order to deal with the problem. Then he would have to uncover some magic or a talisman that would dispel the Mermaids. To do that, he would have to follow them into the water.

As a Demi-God, Hanuman had many powers. As a child he had acquired many boons from gods. Unfortunately, since he had used his new-found powers for mischief a great sage had cursed him, erasing all remembrance of them. When he was commanded to assist Lord Rama the curse was lifted. One power had already served him well in this war - the ability to fly. Another, yet unused, was the ability to survive underwater for a length of time. It was on this that he pinned his hopes as he dove into the water.

He swam with powerful strokes towards the shimmering light which improved visibility under water and turned the sea bed into a floodlit garden.

The floor was carpeted in multi-coloured corals. Fish of all sizes darted in and out, seemingly undisturbed by the activity around them. Hanuman was careful to stay away from the razor sharp edges of the coral reef as he made his way towards the bridge. The bridge was a wonder to behold, floating above him like one of the King's roads that meandered through the countryside. It was broad enough for four horse drawn carts travelling abreast. He took a circuitous route towards the mermaids, who were too preoccupied with the destruction to notice his arrival. Hiding behind a large rocky outcrop, Hanuman observed more closely these fantastic creatures of the deep.

They were playful and terrible to watch. They were childlike as if joyfully breaking down a toy they had built themselves. They tossed the boulders between them in a game of catch. Hanuman noticed subtle differences in their size and shape, and realised that both male and female of the species were present. Some of the larger Mer-People used their strong tails to swat aside rocks and it soon became clear they were competing to see who could throw one the farthest.

Hanuman scanned the assembled crowd trying to decipher a command structure. Who was in charge of the mayhem? He noticed a group floating by the side of the bridge. The Mer-People formed a circle around a Mermaid who was more magnificent than the others. Her strong features were not as severe and her form was lithe. She was bedecked in pearls polished until they reflected the light. Her tail shimmered as if she wore cloth of gold interwoven with precious jewels. A crown of coral was on her lustrous hair, which streamed around her like a cloak. In her hand she grasped a trident.

He had found the Mer-Queen.

So entranced was he by the sight, he did not realise he was no longer hidden behind the rocks. His hulking form was clearly visible to the Mermen guarding their Queen. They gave a shout and swam at him swiftly, brandishing sharp tridents and fixing rocks into slings.

However, they were unprepared for the dexterity and strength of Hanuman, who was no ordinary land-dweller. Calling on his powers he evaded them with ease, navigating the waves better than they did. As he fought off his assailants he glimpsed the Mer-Queen retreating. As he prepared to give chase she turned and called out a command to her guards, waving her trident towards the bridge. Hanuman could not make out her words, but realized she was ordering them to stay and oversee the destruction. Seizing his chance, he swam after her, deeper into the Indian Ocean.

"Who is this half-Man, half-Ape that the powers of the ocean cannot conquer? His strengths are a mystery and I must learn more. He will surely follow me to my lair...

There I will test him and see

where his loyalties truly be..."

CHAPTER SEVEN

The Mer-Queen darted in and out of the sea weed, never quite disappearing from sight. Hanuman suspected that he was being lead somewhere. He was able to survive underwater for sometime longer, but he would have to surface eventually. He did not want to lose her, as she held the key to the Mer-people's mysterious decision to attack his army.

The light was hazy now, but Hanuman discovered this made it easier to follow the swimming figure which shone brighter in the gloom. It was like following a beacon on a foggy night. As he made his way further down, he could see the outline of something vast emerging up ahead.

It was a city underwater. There was no other fitting description. Rocky towers pointed their scraggly fingers accusingly towards the surface. Large caverns opened their mouths to swallow unwelcome visitors. Little lights darted about as the city's denizens made their way through pathways lined with giant sea weed and kelp. Gardens of corals displayed a dash of colour by the openings in the rock. He had been lead into the heart of the Mer-people's land.

Hanuman looked around quickly for the Mer-Queen, who had disappeared from view. He had been so engrossed in the wonder of the place he had taken his eyes off her, and now she was gone. Hanuman turned desperately this way and that, wondering if he should return to the surface. Would he be able to find his way back here if he did?

Then, out of the corner of his eye, he saw her. She was floating at the entrance to a large rocky doorway. She looked directly at him and gestured for him to follow her. Hanuman knew he would need fresh air soon. Yet, he could not forego this opportunity and plunged down.

The opening to the cave shimmered like a curtain. It was a wall of water, unbelievably suspended amidst the water of the ocean. Hanuman tapped it with a finger; it rippled and flexed at his touch. He extended both arms and made his way in.

There was no water inside the cave! It was instead filled with a pocket of air. Hanuman breathed deeply even as his mind registered the impossibility of it all. His eyes adjusted to the gloom as his arms dropped to his short sword still hanging from his side.

The Mer-Queen was reclining on a throne in the centre of the room. She was alone. The throne itself was astonishing, made of white bone and glossy pearls. As he grew more accustomed to his surroundings Hanuman noticed there was no source of light in the cave. The walls were inlaid with reflective glass that shone in the glow of the Mermaid's tail.

As his eyes returned to the Mer-Queen Hanuman noticed that she was speaking. Miraculously, his ears were still stuffed with the leather rolls and he could not make out her words. He hesitated. Should he risk being caught in her spell? Deciding any information he gathered would be worth the risk, he asked, "If I remove these will you promise not to sing your song of sleep?"

She gestured in agreement. The Mer-Queen observed him with a smile as he removed the hastily constructed ear plugs. "That was a clever, and simple, deterrent, Ape Man," she said. "If all land dwellers were like you, our task would be much harder." Her voice was husky, and sang of the depths of the ocean."Do you approve of my private chamber?" she continued, swishing her tail.

"Why have you brought me here?" inquired Hanuman, ignoring her question.

Her laughter was a chorus of tinkling water and roaring waves.

"Why did you follow?" she countered. "I did not lead you on a leash!"

"Why are your people hindering our work?" asked Hanuman, determined not to give in.

"Why are your people invading our sea?" Her eyes glinted as she spoke, but she seemed to be enjoying the game.

"I am weary of this, Lady. What is your name?" asked Hanuman, growing impatient.

The Mer-Queen tossed her hair and sat up. Her eyes were as hard as diamonds, her voice scathing. "You would know my name? Does a mere land creature such as yourself dare to approach one of the most magnificent and intelligent beings to rule the water? Those who follow us to our dwelling place never leave. Beware that your curiosity and insolence does not lead you to a watery grave!"

Hanuman bristled with rage. "I go where I wish, and do what I dare! I have seen and heard enough. The Demon Raavana has obviously struck some bargain with you so as to enlist your help. The details are unimportant. I am Hanuman, Son of the Wind God and blessed with many strange powers that you do not want to test! We were unprepared for your assault before, let us see how things turn out tomorrow!"

With that declaration he strode towards the curtain of water; but it had become a wall of glass.

"This insolent creature from the dry wasteland above dares threaten me? He needs a lesson in humility! He knows not who I am, or what I am capable of...

It is time to tighten the noose

To put my talents to good use..."

CHAPTER EIGHT

Hanuman spun around. The Mer-Queen had her hand extended towards the entrance - she had the use of magic!

"You wished to know why I brought you here. A common brute from above," she hissed. "A whim, nothing more. I may regret it, but seeing an Ape evade my personal guard with such agility and grace in the water, I wished to find out more about you." She lowered her arm, but the entrance stayed sealed.

"Then, it was not I who was curious," commented Hanuman as he walked back to the centre of the cave. "Why should I elect to stay and exchange pleasantries, when there is work at hand?"

"You do not have much of a choice!" she laughed, her good humour restored. "And, I am sure you too, on your part, are burning with curiosity to know more of my people."

Hanuman sat on a rock larger and smoother than the rest. She seemed to be in search of entertainment. Perhaps, he could turn that to his advantage. "What would you like to know, Lady? And would you be gracious enough to tell me who I have the pleasure of addressing?"

She seemed pleased. "So, the Ape does have a civil tongue in his head. I am Suvaana, Queen of the Mer-People."

Choosing to ignore the sarcasm, he answered, "I am Hanuman, General of the Vanara Army."

She lifted an eyebrow. "You truly are one of the Ape People, then? I have lived in this ocean all my life and know almost nothing of the wonders of the mainland. Tell me more."

So, Hanuman described his land and his people. "Lord Brahma created us. Our main purpose now is to assist Lord Rama in his quest to rescue his wife, the Lady Sita. We are blessed with many powers, like those possessed by gods and goddesses. We live in the jungles of Kishkindha. We have our own culture and language just as any other species - we are not brutes!" He paused, to gauge her reaction thus far. "There are thousands of us, and we will win the war against the Demons of Lanka!"

She brushed aside the last comment with a dismissive wave of her hand. "We shall speak of the Demons later. Tell me, why is Lord Rama worthy of your loyalty?"

This was an unexpected turn to the conversation. Wondering as to her motivation in this line of questioning, Hanuman replied, "Rama is a prince of Ayodhya. He is virtuous and just. However, as a result of the machinations of his stepmother he, his wife Sita and his brother Lakshmana were exiled to the Dandaka Forest. He roamed the forest living a humble life and providing protection and relief to ascetics being persecuted by Demons. One day, a Demoness called Shurpanakha saw Rama, became enamoured of him, and tried to seduce him. When Rama refused her, she retaliated by threatening his wife. Lakshmana in turn disfigured the face of the Demoness as punishment. This news reached the Demon king Raavana, who was her brother. Raavana tricked and kidnapped Sita and bore her away to his kingdom on Lanka. Although Rama has had to endure great hardship, he remains an honourable prince. I am sworn to assist him, at all cost."

Suvaana seemed amused. "Yes. And the cost has been quite high, hasn't it? I know you lit up the hills as you set fire to Raavana's palace. Swinging a burning torch from your tail, how novel!"

"Yet, you claim to be ignorant of what is happening in the world above yours," commented Hanuman. He rose from his seat and drew his sword again. "Enough with these games! I will humour you no further. Who are you, really, and what do you want?"

As he looked into her face, he saw a struggle of emotions reflected in her eyes. The silence echoed in the cave as they surveyed each other.

Finally, she said, "I know of the doings of Rama and his family because their actions have torn apart mine. Shurpnakha is my father's sister. I am Raavana's daughter!"

"He underestimates the Demon power that courses wildly through my veins. I shall reveal to him my true majesty! He would make a satisfactory plaything to amuse me when days are dull...

Fools who watch not where they tread

Shall find their hearts fill with dread..."

CHAPTER NINE

Suvaana, the Mer-Queen clapped her hands. For a long moment the sound echoed, sustained in the enclosed cave. Then, Hanuman heard the trickling of water. The walls began to ripple as water seeped down and pooled on the floor. Alarmed, he glanced back at the entrance; it was still impassable.

"Do you wish to drown me in this cave?" he demanded. "If you are truly Raavana's daughter and you seek vengeance, then consider this. I am a mere general. My demise may be mourned but the war will yet be fought, and won!"

"My father ordered me to destroy the bridge, a task that required very little effort on our part. But when I saw you in the ocean, I seized my chance, and you were foolish enough to swim right into my lair! Now I have you in my grasp, and do not lie, your loss will be much more significant than you predict," countered Suvaana. She eyed him speculatively, "Or perhaps my father would reward me well if I were to deliver you trussed up like a wild animal to his doorstep!" Then, with another gesture she commanded the water to rise more rapidly in the cave.

Stilling his feelings of trepidation, Hanuman studied her, seeking a weakness. "Are you so much your father's daughter that you have no compassion, or sense of justice? You do not look like your subjects and I understand now it is the Demon blood breeding true. I am glad you are confined to the ocean and cannot spread terror on the land as your father can!"

At this, she laughed. Then she sat upright and her body seemed to lengthen. Her fish tail stiffened and split in two. The golden shimmer dulled. The scales hardened and disappeared. A pair of bronzed legs emerged where the tail had been. She looked almost Human.

"I can walk on land, if I wish," she said as she moved towards him. She was graceful and seemed to flow across the ground, like the water which was her natural element. "I do not think terror is what I wish to spread, though. I prefer awe, and majesty, and Humans and Apes prostrate at my feet!"

Hanuman stared, taken aback. This was unexpected. Her magical prowess was far greater than he had anticipated. Although she now had the use of legs instead of fins, she looked nothing like any land-dweller known to him. She had retained her sharp features and unnatural eyes and hair. He found the half-Human half-Mermaid form simultaneously alluring and repulsive. She was close enough to strike at with his sword, but he could not bring himself to do it. The water had now risen to his waist. He knew he had very little time to bargain with her, and hopefully, change her mind. She would make a powerful ally in the battle against the Demons.

"I am sorry if the battle between Rama and Raavana has brought you sorrow or pain..." he began. But she cut him off with a finger to his lips.

"No, it hasn't. My father and his Demonkind hold very little sway over us Mer-People. We are conveniently forgotten until the need arises, and we prefer it that way. We pay homage to no one, not even Varuna whose sea we inhabit. I made my father no promises. And neither did he to me." She stroked his cheek with a long finger. "His version of the tale was, I admit, somewhat different to the one you shared."

Hanuman tried to speak, but she laid her hand on his shoulder and lifted her face to his. "I do not wish to take any side in this affair. It is none of my concern. I am satisfied with my life ruling the creatures of the sea." She turned away and resumed her seat on the throne. "I do find, however, the thought of owning a pet monkey quite appealing!"

Hanuman gripped his sword tighter. Yet he could not afford to reveal his annoyance. It was what she obviously hoped for. He was also confused. Her moods changed like quicksilver. One moment she had murder in her eyes, and the next a finger to his lips. She obviously took pleasure in baiting others and playing games. He wondered at her true intentions. What had Raavana promised in return for her aid? He did not believe her claims of impartiality. Thinking back, he wondered, how much had she unwittingly revealed? He considered which approach to take next. Should he try to fight his way out? Flatter her? Subdue her and take her with him to use against her father? How far was he willing to go to ensure victory for Lord Rama's cause?

She noticed the conflict in his eyes, and leaned back in her throne as she waited, enjoying the effect she had had on him thus far.

The water was neck-deep now, and Hanuman knew he was running out of time. He did not wish to perish in this enchanted cave when he had a duty to fulfil on land. His life was of little value to himself, but a foolish self-sacrifice at this juncture would jeopardize the entire invasion.

Finally coming to a decision Hanuman waded towards her. "Lady Suvaana, you are the most alluring, splendid creature I have laid eyes upon. You have bewitched me! I would stay with you forever if only I could. But I need fresh air to survive, and one small cave, however beautiful, is a cage when one cannot move with freedom. And I believe you value freedom. Freedom for yourself and your people. As long as Raavana lives he is a threat to you. You claim he spares no thought for you. I find that wholly unlikely! Raavana is not one to waste his resources or hesitate to manipulate that which is of use to him. You may have protected your people thus far, but you cannot endure forever! You have magic, yes, but is it strong enough to counter his Demonic enchantments?"

Drawing closer he took her hands in his. "Come with me to the surface! You are a Queen! Lead your people for our cause and fight for your freedom, and the freedom of Sita who is imprisoned in your father's palace! Come with me!"

"This Ape has a silver tongue! He excites me and it is disturbing to find I admire his courage and spirit. And, there is a drop of truth to what he says...

With clearer eyes do I now see

Could this be my destiny...?"

CHAPTER TEN

Suvaana looked long and hard into his eyes. Then, leaning forward she clasped his face in her hands.

"This is not the seduction I expected! Yet do not doubt that I see through you. All you wish is victory for your precious Rama, and you care not a jot about the fate of me and mine! Yet, you surprise me with your insight, and I must admit there is some truth to what you say. We do desire freedom more than anything else."

The water, which had been collecting swiftly, was now deep enough to swim in. Resting a hand lightly on his shoulder she circled him as he treaded water, kicking effortlessly with her now Human feet. Then, she paused, as if considering what to say next. "My people may question this decision - but I will join with you."

Wrapping her legs around him, she pulled him closer. The kiss she laid on his lips was passionate, but brief. "And, Hanuman, you may regret your decision to side with me! Mer-People are considered fickle in sailor's tales. But remember that I am part Demon and the blood of Shurpnakha runs in my veins too."

Then, with a laugh and a wave of her hand, she stopped the flow of water into the cave. The next moment she had resumed her fish-like form. She dove into the water and swam to the entrance, "Then, come!"

The journey back to the surface was quick. Although they could not speak as they swam, Suvaana pointed out many treasures and wonders of her domain. As they neared the bridge, she held his hand, and drew him close. When they finally reached the surface, she heaved herself onto the remaining structure and addressed her subjects.

"My people! I know you have worked hard this night. Dawn is almost upon us, but I have news! I have conferred with this emissary of Lord Rama, and have decided to support him in this fight! No longer will we live in fear of my father. We will aid the Humans and Vanara to gain their freedom, and in return, we can establish our own - freedom to travel as we wish and live where we would! Henceforth, I renounce all affiliation with the Demon Raavana! Let us work towards his downfall and re-build this bridge!"

Leaving Suvaana to address her followers, Hanuman swam the short distance to the shore. His armour lay where he had discarded it hours back. He dressed and made his way into the camp. The sun was rising, and the dawn chorus was piping from the trees. The sentries who had been asleep when he made his way out, were now back on their feet, looking dazed, but unharmed. He headed for the command tent where Neela, Nala and their lieutenants were sure to have gathered.

They looked at him in surprise as he entered.

"Have you been for an early swim, Hanuman?" inquired Neela, regarding his wet and matted fur.

"Yes, Neela. And it has been productive on many levels."

"The herbs worked only for a short while last night," interrupted Neela. "We have interviewed those who managed to stay awake. We all agree that..."

Hanuman held up a hand. "That is all in the past. Let me share with you my experiences of last night. I have made a new ally who is re-building the bridge even as I speak. They are the spell casters responsible for the enchanted sleep, and they have promised not to deploy that trick against us again. They are Mer-People!"

This announcement was met with shocked glances and murmurs.

"Mermaids?" gasped Nala. "They are the Demons of the ocean! You cannot think of trusting them!"

"I followed the Mer-Queen to her underwater palace," continued Hanuman, undeterred, "and I have bargained with her and she will assist us in our fight against Raavana..."

The next interruption was from Neela. "She will stab you in the back as soon as the opportunity arises! Surely, Hanuman! You have more sense than this?" He narrowed his eyes and studied the Vanara before him. "Unless...she has cast a spell on you... They are known for playing with sailors..."

"And no one leaves their lair unchanged!" added Nala. "You may have risked our entire expedition! Lord Rama placed such faith in you..."

Hanuman's eyes flashed as he took in the disturbed faces of those around him. "I would sacrifice my life for Lord Rama! Do not assume I take this risk lightly!" Then he laughed. "So, it is not impossible for you to stop bickering and join forces against a common enemy! I understand your doubts. I had them myself before committing to this. But think - what magic do we have to counter the powers of Raavana? With Suvaana's assistance we can build this bridge overnight

71

and take the fight to him! Our mandate is to ensure a safe crossing, and this alliance will guarantee success." Seeing the sceptical looks of those before him he added, "I will watch the Mer-Queen and see that nothing untoward happens." He paused, gripped the hilt of his sword, and looked them directly in the eye, "and, I will deal with her swiftly, and surely, at the first sign of betrayal..."

He turned, as a messenger stumbled through the opening to the tent.

"My Lords!" he panted, "there's a...there's a... Lady walking out of the sea... and she is asking for Lord Hanuman! She says she is the Queen of the Mer-People!"

"My noble Mer-folk have accepted my turn of heart. It is now time to conquer Man and Ape on land. My alliance with Hanuman will prove to all the power of the Mer-Queen...!

My regard for him may grow to love

A few days I shall spend above

The future my magic cannot see

My decision made - I am free..."

CHAPTER ELEVEN

Hanuman smiled to himself. Suvaana did know how to make an entrance, and she may well have her wish of seeing Human and Ape fall prostrate before her. He had to force his way through the throng that had gathered at the shore, gaping at the vision of a Mermaid walking out of the ocean. She was dressed in sea weed as a concession towards Human propriety, and looked both wild and beautiful. When he reached her, he took her by the hand and escorted her to meet the leaders of the Army.

Hanuman noted that neither Nala nor Neela knew quite what to make of her, or how to behave in her presence. Nala's bow was the deeper, while Neela stumbled over a mostly incoherent greeting. Hanuman hid a wry smile at the looks of consternation evident on both their faces. The two Vanara lead the way into the command tent, but came to a sudden halt halfway through.

Neela excused himself from their guest and pulled Hanuman into a private discussion. "What seat do we offer her? We have nothing which would suit a Queen!" He paused, cleared his throat and then inquired in a lower whisper, "Is she capable of taking seat like a Human, anyway?"

Amused by the confusion Hanuman replied, "Yes, her transformation is complete.

Do not worry, she looks very different from her Mer-form. I am sure she can take her place just fine."

Their hurried conversation was interrupted by a silvery laugh. Suvaana, who had sensed the discomfort which was thick in the room, had solved the problem of appropriate seating by selecting the most ornately carved armchair available. She gestured grandly and said, "Please, my Lords, join me at this table. We have much to discuss."

Yet Neela would not be so easily deterred. He muttered anxiously under his breath as he moved towards the table with Hanuman, "We need to organise a feast - what do we serve her to eat?!... And, Hanuman, could you please offer her some alternative attire, once this meeting is convened?!"

Suvaana did not take long to charm the Apes gathered at the table. She took quick control of the proceedings, and described the plan that had already been set in motion out on the waves. It did not take her long to quell all initial doubts regarding her motivations, or Hanumans freedom of will in the matter. Soon, the Vanara and the Mer-Queen reached an agreement, which was put in writing by scribes who were hastily admitted into the tent. These were followed by servants bearing great platters of food, heaped with the bounties of both land and sea.

Outside, news of the surprising turn of events spread like wildfire, and the Vanara workers resumed hurling rocks into the Strait, while the Mer-People herded them and tied them together. With their combined effort the bridge was ready by sunset.

When the camp retired for the night, Hanuman and Suvaana strolled along the beach surveying the bridge that now connected Pamban Island to the north of Lanka. Hanuman reflected how regal she looked now clothed in the finest length of cloth that could be found in the camp at such short notice. The 6 yards of soft cloth was nothing like the finery available for ladies of noble birth at the King's palace. Yet, he doubted that any of them could bear themselves with greater dignity.

Although his immediate task of preparing the way for Rama had been accomplished, he was also preoccupied with the

promises he had made - the promise of freedom to Suvaana, and the promise to Neela and Nala that he would ensure her continued goodwill. He was gambling everything on her word, yet he could see no other way forward. He thought of the calculating looks on the commanders' faces as they observed his interactions with the Mer-Queen. He knew they still suspected his motives, and truth be told, it was an uncertainty he himself felt within.

Suvaana glanced at him as she kicked playfully at the sand. She smiled and said, "Although I possess the power, I have not used the ability to change my form before. The feel of this sand beneath my feet is far different to that which we find on the ocean floor."

Hanuman returned her smile. "You will find there are many other wonderful discoveries awaiting you during your time on land. It is a different kind of beauty, but beauty nevertheless."

"Do you speak only of nature now?" she asked, archly.

Hanuman took her hand in his, and kissed it. "I confess, I have discovered new forms of beauty on this expedition, in the most unlikely of places." He paused as he ran his fingers through her long hair. "I am honoured that you have consented to spend a few days with me. Lord Rama is due soon, and I am sure he would like to thank you in person for all that you have done to further his cause."

Suvanna laughed. "Oh, Hanuman! Do you think I chose to betray my father and side with you for the sake of Rama's cause?" She drew his arms around her slender waist and looked up into his eyes. "I sought to bewitch you with my magic, but you beguiled me with your spirit and strength. I have jeopardized everything for you - and you alone!"

As he nuzzled her neck, Hanuman replied, "Then, I will have to ensure that we defeat Raavana once and for all, to ensure your safety, my love."

As their lips met and their bodies entwined, Hanuman acknowledged that his flattering words spoken in desperation in the cave had crystallized into true affection. Feeling her in his arms, her hair blowing wild, almost Human but so much more, his chest tightened. His one hope now was that she truly upheld her end of the bargain and did not betray them to her father. He did not like to dwell on his choices should that ever come to pass.

As for her, Hanuman could never be sure of what grew in her mercurial mind. Whatever the outcome may be, Hanuman resolved to enjoy her company for as long a time as was given to them.

The rest was in the future and in the hands of the gods.

EPILOGUE

Suvaana lived with Hanuman in the war camp until the arrival of Lord Rama and his retinue. Her advanced knowledge of the coastline contributed much towards the invasion of Lanka. On the night before his departure Hanuman promised to return to Pamban Island when his duty to Rama was fulfilled. As the army marched over the bridge Suvaana resumed her mermaid form and watched the procession with her people.

She did not confide in him that she was with child. Her son, whom she named Macchanu, lived as a Merman. Rumours of a mysterious and powerful sea creature who was half Ape and half fish finally reached Hanuman's ears, in the final years of the war. The two met in battle, but were equally matched. When questioned as to his origins Macchanu informed him that he is the son of Hanuman and Suvaana. Although father and son were thus united, Hanuman never saw Suvaana again.

AUTHOR NOTE

Hanuman is a central character in the Indian Epic Ramayana and its various versions. He is also mentioned in several other texts, including the Mahabharata, the various Puranas and some Jain texts. He is a Demi-God with many powers and is still revered by Hindu worshippers worldwide.

This story is inspired by the Ramakien, the Thai version of the Hindu epic. Unlike in Indian adaptations, in South East Asia Hanuman is not celibate. He meets the mermaid Suvannamaccha with whom he produces a son. Their meeting is brief and is not described in great detail.

FURTHER INFORMATION ON THE RAMAYANA

The Ramayana is more than just a fantasy epic. A curious visitor need not look far to discover various places dotting the landscape of Sri Lanka that trace their roots to this story.

Seetha Amman Temple

Located in Seetha Eliya, a small beautiful village, 5 km away from Nuwara Eliya, the temple is small yet beautiful and rich in Hindu architectural detail and painting and statues of Lord Rama, Sitha Devi, Luxshmana, and Hanuman. According to the legend, the river next to the temple is where Sitha bathed. The footprints on the rock next to the river are believed to be of Hanuman.

Sita Kotuwa

According to the legend Sitha Devi was held captive here. It was once the palace of King Ravana's queen, Mandothari's and was surrounded by waterfalls and beautiful streams.

Kothmale

When King Ravana was taking Sitha Devi to SithaEliya in his chariot, she dropped the rice balls King Ravana had given her. Following these Lord Rama was able to discover her whereabouts. In Kothmale you can still find rice balls (SithaGuli) that the locals now use as a cure for stomach disorders and headaches and as a charm that brings prosperity.

Munneswaram Temple

Located in Chillaw, the Hindu Kovil is one of the oldest Hindu temples in Sri Lanka. King Rama is believed to have prayed here to Shiva asking for redemption after killing Ravana who was a priest of the Brahmin caste.

Manavari Temple

Situated 6km north of Chillaw, Manavari is the temple where, as Lord Shiva advised, Lord Rama installed his first lingam.

Dolukanda Mountain

According to legend, Hanuman was asked to fetch herbs from the top of the Himalaya mountain to heal Lord Rama and Lakshmana who were seriously wounded. However, he broke off an entire section of the mountain as he couldn't identify the herb himself. This piece in turn divided into five portions which landed in various parts of the island.

The beautiful rural village located near Hiripitiya is believed to be one of the landing spots of these pieces. The other 4 places are Rumassala in Galle, Ritigala in Habarana Anuradhapura road, Thalladi in Mannar and Kachchativu in the north.

Nilawari

Nilawari is a famous village in Jaffna, with a pilgrimage site that attracts thousands of locals and tourists each year. According to folklore, the underground well was created by Lord Rama when his army faced a water crisis during the war against king Ravana. Lord

Rama shot a magic arrow to the ground and the spring which arose has not dried up until this day.

Laggala

Located in Mathale Laggala is a rural village with natural beauty and historical value. It is believed that Lord Rama's army was first sighted by king Ravana's troops from this location. King Ravana had also meditated and prayed to Lord Shiva from the Laggala rock, as it was the highest peak of his Kingdom.

Dunuvila

Located in Laggala, Dunuvila lake is believed to be the place where Lord Rama killed king Ravanain single combat.

Yahangala

Translated into English as 'Bedrock', Yahangala is believed to be where locals paid their respects to king Ravana after his death. The place which is located along the Mahiyanganaya – Wasgamuwa road is ideal for a hike and offers amazing views of the surrounding area.

Divurumpola

Divurumpola is where Sitha Devi took her oath to prove her innocence and purity through 'Agni Pariksha'. When she walked into the sacrificial fire, Agni, lord of fire, raised her, preventing any harm and proving her innocence.

Ravana Waterfall

The spectacular waterfall situated by the roadside of Ella-Wellawaya road is 1080 feet high. King Ravanais said to have lived in one of the many natural caves near the waterfall.

Kelaniya Buddhist Temple

After the death of King Ravana, his brother Vibheeshana who sided with Lord Rama during the war was crowned as the next king of Sri Lanka. In the temple, you can see ancient murals of Vibheeshana's coronation.

(https://serendivus.com/13-must-visit-ramayana-related-places-sri-lanka/)

ABOUT THE AUTHOR

Nadishka Aloysius is a teacher, actor, author, blogger and mother of two boys. Being a teacher of Drama and English Language with 20 years' experience, and a mother of two sons who love story time, she finds inspiration in the little everyday details of life. All her books are intimately related to life-experiences, and although they are all based in her home country of Sri Lanka they are generic enough for an international audience.

Nadishka loves reading crime fiction and fantasy and this is reflected in her writing. She conducts creative writing workshops and school visits to share her love of literature. As an actor she prefers to play the antagonist since it allows her to explore the darker sides of human nature.

Other books by this author:

Toran and the Alphabet Fairy
Roo, the Little Red Tuk Tuk
Eyesha and the Great Elephant Gathering
Ronan's Dinosaur
Petscapade
Raavana's Daughter

COMING IN 2019 / 2020
**A new series aimed at creating
awareness**

The Fishing Cat who Lost Her Home
The Sea Turtle who Refused to Go
Manny Monkey Saves his Troop

You can follow her on
AMAZON -
https://www.amazon.com/Nadishka-
Aloysius/e/B01M1KIY0R

GOODREADS -
https://www.goodreads.com/author/show/1
7604897.Nadishka_Aloysius

INSTAGRAM - @nadishkaaloysiusbooks

FACEBOOK - @NadishkaAloysiusBooks